Paws, Claws and Frilly Drawers

For Soggy Donkey and

Soggy Monkey – SH

STRIPES PUBLISHING
An imprint of Magi Publications
1 The Coda Centre, 189 Munster Road,
London SW6 6AW

A paperback original
First published in Great Britain in 2009

ISBN: 978-1-84715-061-5

A CIP catalogue record for this book is available from
the British Library.

Printed and bound in Germany.

10 9 8 7 6 5 4 3 2 1

Paws, Claws and Frilly Drawers

Sarah Horne

Life is full of surprises,
and these can come in all shapes and sizes.

Big surprises,

small surprises,

surprises,

surprises,

and the rarest of all ...

impossible-to-believe

surprises.

And just who would
have believed in a talking cat...?

NICE
KITTY

Return of the Von Volavons

"Pencil. Check. Ruler. Check. Calculator... Check." Molly Potsome finished packing her bag for her first day at her new school and sat on the end of her bed. Her eye fell on her neat school uniform hanging from the wardrobe. For the first time she felt a little nervous. *What will school be like tomorrow? Will my teacher be strict? Will I make any new friends?*

Just then, there was a loud noise from outside. Molly ran to the window.

"HONK, HOOONK!"

honked the horn of the most outrageous car she had ever seen. It flew at frightening speed up the country lane and screeched to a halt outside the solid gold gates of the house next door, Palace Von Volavon. The gates swung slowly

open and the car pulled inside.

Molly watched as Mrs Von Volavon heaved herself out of the car, followed by her husband, who began to unload the cases from the boot. A plump little boy tumbled out of the back, then a pinker-than-pink girl who looked about her age.

I'm sure Mimi will be pleased to see them all again, thought Molly.

Mrs Von Volavon had asked Molly to cat-sit while the family went to an exotic island, and Molly had been only too happy to agree. But, as she had soon discovered, Mimi – or Madam Mimi Mew Mew Von Volavon the Third to give her full name – was no ordinary cat.

Molly smiled to herself. Never in a million years would she have thought she'd meet a talking cat who loved to dress up!

Just then, the girl looked up and caught Molly watching her through the window. Molly gave a little wave. The girl stared back for a moment, scowled and poked out her tongue.

"MuuuuuUUUm!

That girl next door is spying on us!" cried Saffron, pointing up at Molly's window.

At that moment, Molly ducked behind the curtain.

Mrs Von Volavon glanced up at Molly's house and sighed. "There's no one there. Do stop telling stories, Saffron."

"Yeah. Stop telling stories, Saffron," taunted Dylan.

"Am NOt!"

"Are TOO!"

"Shut up, both of you," snapped Mrs Von Volavon, as she unlocked the front door and shooed them inside. "Now hurry up and get upstairs. Dylan, it's time for you to start getting ready for bed. And Saffron, I want you to go and wrap your holiday presents. There's one for your teacher, and one for Molly for looking after Mimi."

"Don't see why she should get a present," muttered Saffron.

Mrs Von Volavon chose to ignore this. "Now where is that little fluffball? Mimi, where are you?" she cooed, walking through into the kitchen.

In the living room, Mimi was having a catnap on her pink velvet cushion. On hearing her name, the little white Persian cat slowly opened one eye. Then swiftly closed it again.

Oh, they're back, she thought. *Well, I'm not missing out on my beauty sleep for them.* But just as she was about to doze off, her tummy began to rumble. *It must be dinner time.*

Mimi padded into the kitchen and threaded herself through Mrs Von Volavon's chunky legs. Then she looked from her empty dish to the cupboard where her food was kept and let out her most pathetic mew.

Mrs Von Volavon opened the cupboard. It was empty. "Oh dear," she sighed. "We've run out of Moggy Meat." She looked over at Mr Von Volavon, who was starting to prepare dinner. "You'll just have to have what we're having, Mimi. Fillet steak – what a treat!"

Fillet steak! Mimi turned up her nose and stuck her tail in the air. *I wish Molly was here. I'm sure she'd have some Moggy Meat.* She trotted back to her cushion, a plan starting to form in her mind.

Molly was packing her gym kit when there was a faint tapping at the window.

"Mimi!" exclaimed Molly.

The cat wore a black and white striped jumper, black socks and a black hat and mask. In one paw, she held a torch.

Molly opened the window. The cat jumped nimbly from the window ledge down on to the floor.

"What are you doing here?" asked Molly. "And what are you dressed as?"

"Erm…" said Mimi, a little sheepishly. "I wasn't expecting you to be here. But as you are, I demand—"

"Oh, here we go—" groaned Molly.

"The finest Moggy Meat in all the land. I want it here and I want it NOW!"

"I'm sorry, Mimi, but I don't have any."

"Liar!" said the cat. "I think you just want to keep it all for yourself." She leaped on to the bed and poked her nose into Molly's gym bag.

"Hang on, I know what you are!" cried Molly. "You're a cat burglar—"

"Molly, it's tea time!" called Mum from the landing.

"Quick ... HIDE!" said Molly. She pulled the gym bag over Mimi and pulled the toggle tight.

Mum pushed open the door and peered inside. "Who were you just talking to, Molly?"

"Nobody..." said Molly.

"RRRRRrrrr," growled the bag, shaking furiously.

"Pardon?"

"I mean, er ... RRRRRight, Mum. What's for tea?"

"It's RRRRatatouille!" said Mum.

"YUCK," said Mimi.

"I mean ... YUM! That sounds delicious!" said Molly.

"OK..." said Mum, feeling a little confused. "So, are you ready for school?"

"Help!" went the bag.

"Don't worry, love, it won't be as bad as you think," said Mum. "Tea's on the table in five minutes," she added, as she closed the door behind her.

"Phew, that was a lucky escape," whispered Molly. She undid the toggle. "You can come out now."

Mimi wriggled her way out of the bag.

"I've never been so insulted in all my life," she said, dusting herself down. "First you hide your Moggy Meat from me, then you shove me into a smelly bag ... and then..." She paused, a puzzled expression crossing her face.

"You've forgotten, haven't you, Mimi?"

Mimi gasped theatrically. "That's it! I'm not putting up with this any longer! I'm LEAVING!"

At that, Mimi leaped through the window and was gone.

First Day at School

"Come on, Molly! You don't want to be late for your first day!" shouted Mum, holding open the front door.

"Coming!" cried Molly, hurrying down the stairs and following her mum outside.

At that moment, a scowling girl slammed the golden gates of Palace Von Volavon. She was carrying a large, beautifully-wrapped present.

"Oh look," said Mum. "That must be Saffron Von Volavon. Well, go on, Molly ... say hello."

Molly caught up with Saffron. "Hi, I'm Molly from next door," she said.

"And I'm Pamela Potsome," said Molly's mum.

"Good morning, Mrs Potsome," said Saffron, sweetly. She looked Molly up and down. "Hello, Molly," she added.

"Now why don't you two walk to school together?" said Mum. "It'll give you a chance to get to know each other. Molly's a bit nervous about starting her new school. You can tell her all about it."

"Yes, Mrs Potsome," replied Saffron.

"Great," said Mum. "Have a lovely day!"

Molly waved her mum goodbye, and the two girls started off down the road.

Just then, the gates of Palace Von Volavon clanged shut, and a small, round boy waddled after them.

"WAIT FOR ME!" he shouted.

"Oh, this is my pesky little brother, Dylan," said Saffron.

"Hello, Dylan," said Molly. Dylan pulled his finger from his nose and waved.

Saffron rolled her eyes.

"Gosh," said Molly, looking at the big present under her arm. "Who's that for?"

Saffron narrowed her eyes. "Not telling."

Molly read the label on the top of the present. "Oh, it's for Mrs Grey. I'm in her class, too!" she said.

"Really," said Saffron. "Well, I'm her favourite pupil."

"Saff-RON!" piped up Dylan. "What about Molly's present?"

Saffron shot her brother a poisonous look and shoved Mrs Grey's present into his arms. She then reluctantly removed a shell bracelet from her wrist and dropped it into Molly's hands. "This is for you. For looking after Mimi," she muttered.

"Thank you," said Molly, putting it on. "It's beautiful."

"Now, let me tell you about Fuffleton Primary..." said Saffron in a hushed voice. **"IT'S HAUNTED!"**

"Really?" said Molly.

"A hundred years ago, there was a boy called Johnny and one day—"

"Don't talk about Ice Cream Johnny again," said Dylan, putting his hands over his ears.

"One day," continued Saffron, "he was running in the corridor, when he slipped on a puddle of ice cream, banged his head and DIED!" she said dramatically.

"Oh no," said Molly, going along with the story.

"His ghost haunts the corridor to this very day," said Saffron.

"Ice Cream Johnny... Scary," said Molly, not believing a word of it.

Saffron continued to tell Molly far-fetched stories the rest of the way to school. By the time the three of them reached the gates, the other children were already lining up noisily in the playground, ready to go into class.

Molly followed Saffron and joined the back of the line for Mrs Grey's class.

The children shuffled through the door into a large, bright classroom. Everyone sat down, ready for the lesson to begin. Molly hovered by the door, suddenly feeling nervous.

"Mrs Grey," said Saffron sweetly, trotting up to her teacher, "I brought you a present from my holiday."

"That's very kind of you, Saffron," said Mrs Grey, putting the present on her desk. "I'll open it later." Then she spotted Molly. She smiled warmly and beckoned her over.

The whole class clapped, apart from Saffron. *Mrs Grey ignored my present,* she sulked. *And it's all Molly's fault.*

"Now, Molly," said Mrs Grey. "Let's find you a seat. Oh, look. There's a spare place next to Saffron."

As Molly went and sat down, Saffron turned her head away and looked in the opposite direction.

Mrs Grey took the register, and then it was time for the first lesson. "Now please take out your maths books and your pencils and we'll make a start."

Saffron fumbled in her pink pencil case and pulled out a bright pink felt tip.

"Just need to test out my pen," she said, then scribbled all over Molly's brand-new exercise book.

During the course of the lesson, Saffron managed to snap Molly's ruler in half and break her calculator by dropping it on the floor, then accidentally treading on it. Molly was glad when it got to break time.

As soon as she entered the playground, a group of her classmates rushed over.

"Hi, Molly!" said Jane. "Do you want to play ponies with us?"

"Yes, I love ponies!" said Molly, smiling.

Saffron stood on her own in the middle of the playground, glowering at the crowd of children around Molly.

"Huh! Thinks she's Miss Popular, does she!" Saffron sneered. "Well, I'll show her."

Chapter Three

Mrs Grey's Surprise

"OK, class," said Mrs Grey, as the children sat down at their tables after break. "I have a surprise for you. On Thursday it's Bring Your Pet to School Day!"

The whole class erupted into excited babble.

"Wow! COOL. I'm bringing Bongo!" said Jane.

"I'm bringing Rover!" cried Brian.

"I'm bringing Misty!" said Jasmine excitedly.

Saffron climbed up on her chair.

I'M BRINGING LADY!
The most beautiful pony
in ALL THE WORLD!

"Saffron," said Mrs Grey. "I've told you before about shouting. And get down off that chair right now! I'm taking a star from your chart."

Molly watched as Saffron sat back in her seat.

"What are you looking at?" hissed Saffron.

"Nothing," said Molly, staring down at the table.

"Here's how the day will work," Mrs Grey continued. "The pets will take part in some of our morning lessons. Then in the afternoon there will be a Pet Parade. This will take place in the school hall and all your parents are invited. At the end of the parade there will be a prize for the BEST PET!"

The children whispered excitedly to each other. Suddenly Molly felt worried. *What am I going to do?*

Mrs Grey caught Molly's eye and smiled. "And it doesn't matter if you don't have a pet, you can bring a favourite teddy instead.

"Now, everybody has a part to play in the Pet Parade. Brian, you and Harry can do the music. Jasmine and Jane, you can take care of the decorations. And who wants to be in charge of the costumes?"

Saffron's hand shot up. "Mrs Grey, Mrs Grey, I'm EXCELLENT at costumes."

"Costumes, Saffron Von Volavon. And who wants to help Saffron?"

For once, the class was silent.

"Don't be shy," said Mrs Grey. "What about you, Molly? You and Saffron are neighbours, aren't you? So I'm sure you must be good friends by now."

"Of course, Mrs Grey," said Molly.

"HMMPH!" said Saffron.

Saffron continued to be a pain for the rest of the day. She bumped into Molly in the lunch queue, making her spill her soup, then tripped her up with a skipping rope in games.

Molly couldn't wait to get home. Luckily, Saffron had to go to ballet straight after school, so Molly didn't have to walk back with her.

"How was your first day at school?" asked Dad at teatime.

"It was ... OK," said Molly quietly. "The girls in my class seem friendly. Well, most of them... But..."

"But?" said Dad, raising his eyebrows.

"It's Bring Your Pet to School Day on Friday, and I've been paired up with Saffron Von Volavon to do the costumes, and she wasn't very nice to me. And, what's more, I don't have a pet!"

"But Saffron seemed like such a sweet little girl when I met her this morning," mused Mum. "I went round to see Mrs Von Volavon's holiday snaps this afternoon. She was saying how lovely it is that Saffron now has someone next door to play with."

Molly brightened up a little. "Maybe Saffron was just having a bad day."

"We all have them," said Dad. "And I'm sure some of the other children in your class don't have pets either."

"I guess so," said Molly. "Mrs Grey said we can bring a teddy if we don't have a pet."

"Why don't you take Philip?" suggested Dad.

"I suppose I could take Philip..."

"Tomorrow will be different, you'll see," said Mum, exchanging looks with Dad.

Chapter Four

Supper at the Von Volavons

The next morning, when Molly came downstairs, there was a pink envelope lying on the doormat with her name on it. She opened it and started to read:

Saffron Von Volavon
Requests the
pleasure of your company
for supper
This evening at the Palace Von Volavon.
Five o'clock sharp.
Be late at your peril!

Tea at the Von Volavons...? But I thought Saffron hated me yesterday! Molly tried to look on the bright side. *Well, at least I'll get the chance to see Mimi again.*

"I've been invited over to tea next door tonight," said Molly, as she waved her mum goodbye on the doorstep. "Did you have something to do with this?"

Mum just smiled. "How nice. Look, there's Saffron and Dylan now."

Molly sighed and hurried to catch up. "Thanks for inviting me to tea," she said.

"I didn't," replied Saffron.

"I thought the mums had something to do with it," said Molly cheerfully.

"My mum's always making me do things I don't want to," muttered Saffron.

Oh dear, it looks like Saffron is having another bad day, thought Molly.

Things didn't improve when they got into class, either.

"OK, children, today we're going to start getting ready for the Pet Parade," announced Mrs Grey. "So if you could get into your pairs, please, I'll get the materials out."

Molly turned to Saffron. "Have you got any ideas for costumes yet?"

"Maybe..." said Saffron mysteriously.

"How about 'Dress as your Pet'? That could be fun."

A thin smirk spread across Saffron's face. "HA! That's the stupidest idea I've ever heard!"

Molly bit her lip.

"Well, have you got any better ideas?"

"Of course I have," said Saffron. "But I'm not telling you."

Just then, Mrs Grey appeared. "Oh, girls. Before I forget, you might need this," she said, placing a key on the table. "It's for the dressing-up cupboard."

"I'll take that!" said Saffron, snatching the key and popping it into her pocket.

Molly watched as Saffron got out a pink notebook and started to write, her tongue sticking out in concentration. "Stop trying to copy me," said Saffron, shielding her notebook with her arms.

"But we're supposed to be working together," pointed out Molly.

"I don't need you. I know everything there is to know about dressing up. In fact, I'm the best dresser-upper in the whole world!"

Molly smiled to herself. *Oh no you're not. I know someone much better!*

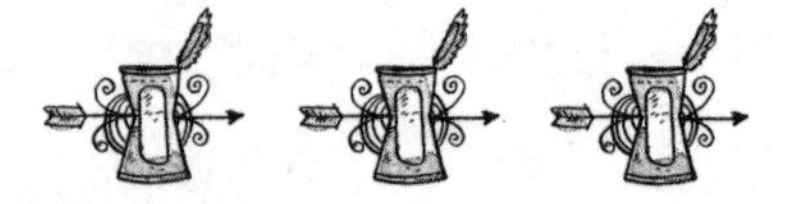

After school, Molly trudged through the golden gates of Palace Von Volavon, past the grand fish fountain and up to the front door. She had managed to avoid walking home with Saffron by staying behind to talk to Mrs Grey, but there was no getting out of going round for tea. She knocked on the door.

Maybe Saffron will act differently when she's not at school, she thought, hopefully.

"Come in," called the voice of Mrs Von Volavon.

Molly tiptoed inside. "Hello?" she called.

"Hello. Oh, it's you," came a familiar voice from behind her. It was Mimi.

"Hi, Mimi. I've come for tea," whispered Molly.

"Tea?" mewed the cat. "I only eat Moggy Meat these days. Have you ever tried–"

The cat fell silent as Mrs Von Volavon poked her head round the kitchen door.

"Why, hello, Molly. Has Saffron not come down yet?"

Molly shook her head.

"SAAAffron! Dylan!

Come down, Molly's here and tea's ready," Mrs Von Volavon hollered up the stairs.

Mrs Von Volavon turned to Molly. "Come this way, please, Molly."

She led Molly through into a room she had never been in before and Molly found herself standing in front of the longest table she had ever seen.

"Now, you sit here," said Mrs Von Volavon, pulling out a chair.

There was the sound of thumping feet as Dylan ran down the stairs. He hurtled into the dining room and took his place at the top of the table.

Finally, Saffron strolled into the room.

"You can sit opposite Molly, darling," said Mrs Von Volavon. "I'm sure you two have lots to talk about."

"No," said Saffron under her breath, as her mother left the room.

Saffron sat down. She glared at Molly from across the table.

Molly looked around awkwardly. Suddenly, out of the corner of her eye, she saw a flash of white fur.

It was Mimi.

Molly let out a gasp as the cat leaped on to a beautiful mahogany cabinet full of trophies and tried to scramble to the top.

"What's the matter?" asked Saffron.

"Oh, nothing," Molly replied, keeping her eye on Mimi as she heaved herself on to the top of the cabinet, almost knocking a huge vase to the floor with her tail.

"Look, it's Mimi," said Dylan. "Here puss, puss, puss..."

Ignoring him, Mimi started to lick her paw.

"I did enjoy looking after Mimi while you were on holiday," said Molly, glancing over at Mimi and giving her a wink. "She's lovely..."

"Not really. She's a little fleabag, a silly moggy, a mangy CAT," said Saffron, folding her arms. "My pony is much better..."

Mimi glowered angrily. Somebody had said the C-A-T word.

The door swung open and Mrs Von Volavon walked through with three silver dishes.

"Here we are my darlings!" she said, placing the dishes on the table. "Beans marinated in fresh tomatoes on a platter of toasted bread."

"Yum," said Molly. "Beans on toast, my favourite."

There was an awkward silence.

Then...

SMASH!

"Oh you little powder-puff pain in the neck!" screeched Mrs Von Volavon, spotting Mimi on top of the cabinet. "That vase was priceless. Come down here this instant!" She marched over, grabbed Mimi by the scruff of the neck and dragged her from the room.

"Hey, Saffron!" whined Dylan, looking over at his sister's plate. "You've got more than me!"

"Have NOT."

"Have TOO."

"Anyway," said Saffron, turning to Molly. "I was telling you about my pony. She's called Lady, and she is the most amazing pony ever!"

"But, Saffron, you haven't got a pony yet," Dylan piped up. "Dad said you have to wait till your birthday."

"*QUIET*, YOU!" snarled Saffron, kicking him under the table.

So Saffron doesn't have a pony after all, thought Molly, cheering up a bit.

Saffron and Dylan continued to bicker throughout dinner, but at least it meant Molly didn't have to talk to Saffron.

"Thank you, Mrs Von Volavon," said Molly, as she finished off her choc ice. "The beans marinated in fresh tomatoes on a platter of toasted bread were delicious. And the ice cream smothered in a chocolate crust was the nicest I've ever had."

Saffron leaped up from her seat.

"Where are you going?" said Mrs Von Volavon, as she gathered up the plates.

"I've got to ... do my homework," said Saffron desperately. "Bye, Molly!"

"Poor darling, don't work too hard," said Mrs Von Volavon. She turned to Molly. "I suppose it's time for you to go home. It's been lovely having you. Do come again."

Molly smiled politely. *Not likely,* she thought.

Chapter Five

Mimi Meets a Lady

As soon as Molly had left, Saffron ran downstairs to her father's study and burst through the door.

"Daaadddy..." said Saffron sweetly.

"Hmmm?" said Mr Von Volavon, looking up from his paper.

"You know you said I could have a pony on my birthday. Well..."

Saffron paused.

"I WANT MY PONY *NOW!*" she screeched. "We've got Bring Your Pet to School Day on Friday and I need to win the Best Pet Prize."

"What about your goldfish?" said Mr Von Volavon.

"*NO*. I WANT A PONY," said Saffron.

"Or you could ask Dylan if you can borrow his guinea pigs."

"What, Moo Moo and Dinky?" said Saffron in disgust.

"I know ... how about Mimi?" said Mr Von Volavon, pointing at the cat, who was standing in the doorway.

"What, that waste of space?" huffed Saffron. "She's just a fleabag with legs! A fluffball with eyes! A moggy with mange! A pathetic *CAT!* And a very boring one at that!" sneered Saffron. "If I take her, I will lose. And I never lose!"

Mangy? Pathetic? Fleabag… CAT? Mimi couldn't believe her ears. "Nobody speaks about Madam Mimi Mew Mew Von Volavon the Third like that! I'll get you for this, Saffron," she hissed under her breath.

The next morning there was a commotion next door. Molly leaped out of bed and ran to the window. A huge horsebox was reversing into Palace Von Volavon's driveway.

Oh no! What am I going to do? thought Molly. *Saffron really has got a pony for the Pet Parade, and I have … Philip the teddy. I'm going to be laughed out of Fuffleton.*

Molly got dressed and trudged miserably downstairs.

"What's the matter?" asked Dad.

"Saffron has a pony," mumbled Molly, sitting down for breakfast. "The most beautiful pony in all the world. And I don't have a pet for Thursday."

"Don't worry, love," said Mum. "I'm sure we can work something out."

"My pony, Lady, is the fairest, most wonderful prancing pony in all the world," said Saffron, as she skipped along to school.

"You're very lucky," said Molly.

"You don't have a pet, do you?" said Saffron. "You'll just have to bring a teddy bear or something..."

Molly blushed.

"You *are* bringing a teddy!" Saffron sniggered. "What a baby!"

Saffron continued to tease Molly about her teddy throughout the morning. After lunch, the children carried on preparing for the Pet Parade. To Molly's relief, Saffron went off at once to the dressing-up cupboard to plan her costume in secret.

Molly watched as Jane and Jasmine cut shapes out of coloured paper.

"Do you need any help?" she asked.

Meanwhile, back at Palace Von Volavon Mimi was trying to have a catnap when she heard a strange noise from the garden.

What is that horrible racket? she thought sleepily.

But then her curiosity got the better of her and she decided to investigate.

She trotted to the cat flap and out into the back garden. The grass felt soft beneath her paws, then squelchy.

Mimi looked down...

To her horror she found herself tummy-deep in a huge, very smelly pile of poo.

"POO-EY!" said Mimi, curling up her nose. It was the most disgusting thing she had ever smelt. "Look at my beautiful fur. It's ruined! Who is responsible for this?"

Mimi turned round.

Towering above her was the biggest creature she'd ever seen.

"Was this you?" Mimi glowered, pointing at the poo with one paw. "You should be ashamed of yourself. I mean, haven't you heard of a litter tray?"

The pony munched peacefully on her hay and didn't say a word.

“Explain yourself!” demanded the cat.

The pony shook her beautiful mane and snorted through her nose.

“Well, I’m not wasting any more of my time talking to a rude, ignorant creature with no table manners,” said the cat, turning her little pink nose in the air and marching back into the house to clean herself up.

To Molly’s surprise, school had been much better today. It was fun helping Jane and Jasmine with the decorations. Saffron had spent most of the afternoon in the dressing-up cupboard, which had suited her just fine.

Molly was looking through the box that Mrs Grey had given them for making the decorations. It was brimming with coloured paper, sequins, spangles, feathers and glitter. Suddenly inspiration struck. *I can make the animal costumes!* thought Molly. *Then I won't need the dressing-up cupboard at all! All I need is some ears, masks and tails. And I'm sure I've got some face paints at home, too.*

But would they be ready in time?

Molly turned to Jane and Jasmine, who were just finishing off the last of the paper chains.

"Would you mind helping me make some animal masks and ears?" she asked.

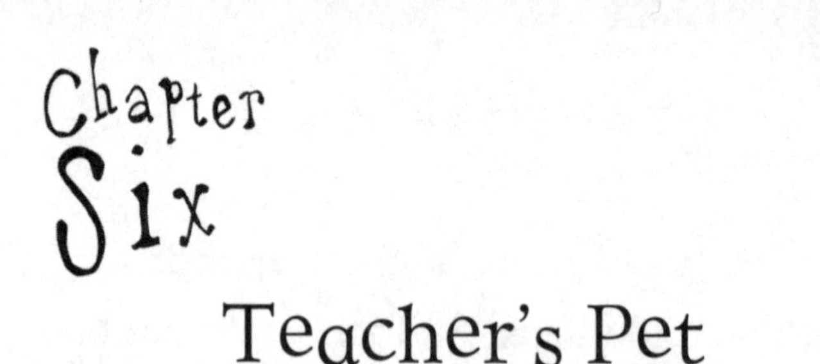

Teacher's Pet

It was Thursday morning and Molly woke with a start. The dreaded day had arrived. Even with Jane and Jasmine's help she hadn't finished the costumes for the Pet Parade – no thanks to Saffron. And she still didn't have a pet.

"Time to get up, sleepyhead," Mum called up the stairs. "I've got a surprise for you. It's waiting outside."

Molly quickly got dressed, wolfed down her breakfast and ran out into the front garden.

"Oh, look!" gushed Mum. "How thoughtful, they've dressed her up ready for Bring Your Pet to School Day!"

Her? Dressed up? thought Molly. It couldn't be...?

She looked down and there, sitting on the path, was Mimi, dressed in a pristine school uniform.

"What are you doing here?" whispered Molly, as her mum went back into the house.

"Waiting for you. I'm ready for school," mewed the cat.

"I can see that," said Molly, taking in Mimi's satchel and hockey stick.

Well, at least I've got a pet, thought Molly. *But what will Saffron think of me borrowing the family cat? And what if Mimi misbehaves? This day could be a cat-astrophe!*

Mum appeared holding a cat carrier. "Mrs Volavon gave me this to carry Mimi," she said. "Now, help me get her inside otherwise you'll be late."

Mimi's back arched and her tail fluffed up. "Oh no you don't," she hissed.

"Can't you stop this thing swinging about? I'm starting to feel travel sick," said Mimi.

"Well, if it wasn't for you I wouldn't be late and I wouldn't have to run," said a breathless Molly, as she dashed up to the school gates.

It had taken two cans of Moggy Meat and a good shove to get Mimi into the cat carrier, and she had complained the whole way to school.

"Are you going to let me out now?" asked Mimi, as Molly walked into the bustling playground.

"Not just yet," said Molly.

There were cats. There were dogs. There were rabbits. There were hamsters. There was even a goat.

"Yucky. Disgusting. Quite nice fried. Delicious..." muttered Mimi, as she surveyed the animals through the bars of her cat box.

"Now, Mimi, you've got to promise not to eat any of them!" said Molly firmly. "I'm sure none of them are nearly as delicious as Moggy Meat," she added.

"Giddy up!" said a voice from behind them. "I said GIDDY UP."

Molly turned to look.

It was Saffron on Lady.

She was just steering her pony towards the school doors when Mrs Grey hurried over. "Now Saffron, that's a lovely pony. But I don't think you can bring her inside."

"But Mrs Grey! WHY not?" moaned Saffron.

"She's just too big. She'll have to graze on the playing field. I'm sure she'll be much happier there. We can all come and see her later," said Mrs Grey firmly.

The rest of the children filed into the classroom, as Saffron went to take Lady to the field.

"Good morning, children ... and pets," said Mrs Grey.

"Good morning, Mrs Grey," chanted the class, as everyone crowded into the room.

"Welcome to Bring Your Pet to School Day. Today we're going to have a lot of fun! Our lessons this morning will be a bit different to usual, as you'll soon see. Then after lunch you can get ready for the Pet Parade. I've asked your parents to arrive at two."

Mrs Grey looked at the rows of smiling faces. "So, who would like to introduce their pet first?"

Everyone stuck up their hand.

"Miss," whined Saffron. "How can I introduce Lady if she's outside?"

"Don't worry, Saffron," Mrs Grey said patiently. "Once everyone else has presented their pet, we'll go and meet your pony. Right. Now, let's start with you, Jasmine... Come up to the front, please."

"This is my rabbit, Misty. She likes to eat carrots and lettuce," said Jasmine, holding up her rabbit.

"What lovely soft fur," said Mrs Grey,

giving Misty a stroke. Jasmine then returned to her seat.

"Now Brian, what about your pet?"

"This is my dog, Rover, and he can do a special trick!" said Brian, making his way to the front. He almost lost his balance as the large, boisterous dog tugged on his lead.

"Great! But let's save special tricks for the Pet Parade," said Mrs Grey. "And Jane...?"

Jane held up a seemingly empty cage. "This is Bongo my hamster. I think he's asleep at the moment."

"Ah," said Mrs Grey. "Perhaps he'll wake up later on."

Molly began to shrink down into her seat, as she watched the children introduce their pets one by one.

Please don't pick me, she thought in panic. *Mimi's bound to be difficult after I've kept her locked in a cat box all morning.*

Mrs Grey looked around the classroom.

"It's my turn, Miss," said Saffron, jumping to her feet.

"In a minute, Saffron. We've still got Molly. Do you want to bring your pet to the front, Molly?"

Molly gulped.

She stood up and walked slowly to the front of the class, carrying the cat box. She set the box on the desk and undid the catch...

"This is Mimi," said Molly brightly.

No cat appeared.

"Mimi, are you going to come out? Please," whispered Molly.

Still nothing happened.

"Mimi, if you don't behave you won't get any Moggy Meat for lunch," said Molly under her breath.

There was another pause. Then Mimi popped her head through the door. She looked around, poked out one white paw, then another... Finally, she squeezed the rest of her body through the entrance. Perching on her hind paws at the edge of the desk, she took in the rows of open-mouthed faces.

"She's wearing clothes!" whispered Jane.

"A school uniform!" exclaimed Jasmine.

"COOOOL," said Harry.

"WOW," said Emma.

"She's standing on her back legs. What a brilliant trick!" said Brian. "How did you teach her to do that?"

"Bravo, Molly!" smiled Mrs Grey. "I have to say, I'm very impressed that you've been thoughtful enough to dress her up! And she's so well trained! A gold star for effort!"

Molly blushed. The whole class clapped. All except for Saffron, that is.

Saffron's face turned a violent shade of salmon pink.

"Saffron, what have I told you about telling stories," said Mrs Grey firmly. "Molly, you can go back to your table."

To her surprise, Mimi returned to the cat box without a fuss. Avoiding catching Saffron's eye, Molly went and sat down.

"Oh dear, we've been having so much fun it's break time already," said Mrs Grey, looking at the classroom clock. "Sorry, Saffron, we'll just have to meet Lady later. Class, you can all take your pets into the playground for a runaround."

Chapter Seven

Art Attack!

"Not so fast," said Saffron, catching up with Molly as she walked into the playground. She pushed her face up against Molly's. "You stole my CAT."

"Saffron, I didn't steal your cat. Your mum agreed with my mum that I could borrow her for the day," said Molly, taking a step backwards. "What about your new pony?"

"I didn't get the chance show her to the class, thanks to YOU!"

Molly thought on her feet. "But just think how impressed everyone will be when they get to see you ride Lady at the Pet Parade."

A smile crept across Saffron's face. "You're right. And Lady IS going to win the Best Pet Prize." She looked down at the cat box. "She's far better than that little fleabag, Mimi."

When the children and their pets came back after break the desks were covered in newspaper. That could mean only one thing: ART.

"Right, class," said Mrs Grey. "Because it's Bring Your Pet to School Day we're having a slight change from our usual timetable. I want you to paint portraits of your pets."

The children burst into excited whispers. All except for Saffron.

"But Miiisssss," she whined. "How can I paint a portrait of Lady if she's outside?"

Mrs Grey smiled patiently. "Well, if you sit at that table by the window, you should be able to see your pony from there. I think a picture of Lady in a field will be lovely, don't you?"

"Suppose so," shrugged Saffron.

"Come and line up for your paints and brushes, please," said Mrs Grey.

Molly gathered what she needed from the art cupboard and returned to her table. She reached for the cat box.

It was empty.

"Oh no!" gasped Molly. "I mustn't have shut the box properly."

Molly stared at her blank canvas. *Where was that cat? She could be getting up to all sorts of mischief by now.*

Just then, out of the corner of her eye, she saw Mimi pad across the room. The cat was now wearing a beige artist's smock and a perfectly placed black beret.

Mimi jumped on to the chair next to her.

"Where have you been, Mimi?" whispered Molly. "And what ARE you wearing?"

"One needed to change one's outfit," said Mimi grandly. She took a brush in her paw. "An artist needs a model and I suppose you'll do. Now if you could sit still then I can begin."

"Begin what?"

"Painting your portrait, of course," replied the cat. "Isn't that what we're supposed to be doing?"

"Well, how about we take turns?" said Molly. "If you pose for me, then you can have a go afterwards. I'm sure you'll be a wonderful model."

"How about this?" said Mimi, striking her most elegant pose.

When it came to Mimi's turn, Molly had never seen the cat quite so focused. *Maybe Mimi has a hidden talent,* she thought.

Finally, Mimi stepped back to admire her work.

"Can I see?" asked Molly, coming over to look at her portrait.

Suddenly, Mrs Grey appeared behind them. She leaned over to study the painting. "Gosh! Goodness, how very ... creative," she said. "I wasn't expecting anything quite so abstract."

Mrs Grey looked at the clock. "Class, I want you to stop painting now and tidy up," she announced. "We must get on with our history lesson."

Molly started to collect up the brushes, placing them in the water jar.

"Sit still," ordered Mimi. "I haven't finished your hair."

"Come on, Mimi, I need to tidy up."

Mimi tried to snatch back a brush, but Molly pulled it away and her paw plunged straight into the water jar.

"REAOOOOOOOW!" howled Mimi. "My paw – it's all WET and COLD."

"Let me have a look," said Molly, reaching for the little cat.

Mimi jumped from the chair and bolted across the floor.

"MIMI, NO!" cried Molly, as the cat leaped on to Jane's table.

"ARRGH!" yelled Jane.

Mimi shot Molly a 'you can't catch me look'. But suddenly the little cat's face fell, as something wet seeped into her fur. She was sitting in a palette of blue paint!

Mimi gazed in horror at her blue bottom and tail.

"Molly, can you please catch your cat and take her to the bathroom for a wash," said Mrs Grey. "Then you can take her straight to the hall where Mr Binkey the caretaker will be looking after all the pets for the next lesson."

Molly reached out for Mimi, but the cat was too fast for her.

No one washes me, thought Mimi, haring off.

The classroom door was shut. But then Mimi spotted the open window above Saffron's desk. She scampered under the tables, threading her way between children's legs, then jumped...

Saffron looked up to see a blue-bottomed cat flying towards her.

"ARRRGH! Get that horrible flea-ridden cat away from me!" she screeched, as she ducked out of the way.

Mimi landed on the desk and swished her paint-stained tail crossly. All over Saffron's painting. Then, forgetting about her escape attempt, she sprang to the ground and started licking her paw.

"Mrs Grey, my painting's ruined!" cried Saffron.

"Oh Saffron, did you spill the paint? You really should be more careful," said the teacher, looking over.

"It wasn't me, Miss, it was Mimi!"

Mrs Grey sighed. "What have I told you about making up stories, Saffron?"

Molly finally caught up with Mimi, and bundled the cat into the carrier. "Right, Mimi, you're coming with me."

"I'll get that cat for this," Saffron muttered. "And you, Molly Potsome."

Chapter Eight

Cleocatra

By the time Molly had taken Mimi to the school hall and got back to the classroom, the history lesson was already in full swing.

Mrs Grey looked up. "Just to recap for Molly – today we're looking at the Ancient Egyptians. Now, who can tell me about Cleopatra?"

There was silence around the room.

"Anybody?" said Mrs Grey. "Well, Cleopatra—" The teacher stopped in her tracks as her eye fell on a very strangely-dressed cat. Molly gasped.

"That's Cleopatra!" shouted Brian, pointing at Mimi.

"Cleo-CAT-tra more like!" suggested Jasmine. The whole class laughed.

"She looks just like the picture!" said Jane, holding up her history book.

Mimi was wearing an enormous black wig, a golden headdress and jewelled collar, and very wobbly eye make-up. In her paw was a green snake staff.

"You're for it **NOW**," whispered Saffron to Molly. "You're not supposed to have your pet in class."

A smile crept across Mrs Grey's face. "How inventive, Molly! Mimi is a great visual aid. I think you deserve another gold star for that. Now, do you know cats were worshipped as gods in Ancient Egypt?"

I like the sound of that, thought Mimi.

"Mrs Grey, that's MY cat! The gold star should be MINE," protested Saffron, rushing up to the front of the class. She reached out to grab Mimi, but the cat leaped to the floor and disappeared under one of the tables.

"Saffron, I told you earlier about telling fibs. Now go and sit down."

Saffron walked back to her table. At that moment, with perfect timing, a little paw shot out from under a table right into Saffron's path, sending her flying.

She landed in a crumpled heap in the story corner, showering books everywhere.

The class broke into laughter.

Saffron fumed silently from under a pile of books.

Cleocatra grinned fiendishly.

For the rest of the lesson, Cleocatra sat quietly on top of the desk, while Molly filled in a worksheet about Ancient Egypt.

"Time to stop writing now," said Mrs Grey. "As it's a special day, we're going to do something different this lunchtime. First you're going to go into the school hall to feed your pets, and then the dinner ladies have prepared packed lunches for you all."

Saffron raised her hand.

"Saffron, you can go and feed Lady in the field first, then join us," said Mrs Grey. "Please wait here for Mr Binkey to take you over. Children, if you can collect your pet food and follow me."

As the classroom emptied, Saffron sat and sulked.

I WILL win the Best Pet Prize. I'll show Molly and that fleabag cat. NOBODY BEATS SAFFRON VON VOLAVON!

Just then, she spotted her holiday present, still unopened on Mrs Grey's desk. Saffron grinned as a dark plot formed in her devious mind.

She picked up the present and poked her head round the classroom door.

There was no one around.

If I'm quick I've got just enough time to get away before Mr Binkey turns up, she thought.

She slipped the dressing-up cupboard key from her pocket and hurried off down the corridor.

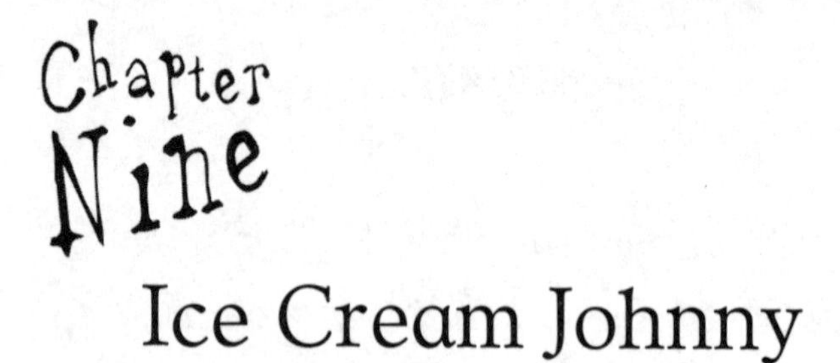

Ice Cream Johnny

Molly filed into the school hall with the other children, but when she looked down Mimi was no longer by her side. She wasn't too worried. Mimi was bound to be back soon if there was food to be had.

Sure enough, the moment Molly started to open a can of Moggy Meat, Mimi appeared by her side.

"Dressing for dinner were you, Mimi?"

asked Molly, as she took in the cat's evening gown.

"Naturally," said Mimi.

Mimi was just tucking into her Moggy Meat when Rover came and stuck his nose in her bowl.

"Sorry!" cried Brian, running over to grab the dog's lead.

Mimi hissed and her fur stood on end.

"I think we should get out of here before someone gets hurt," said Molly. "Don't worry, I've got more Moggy Meat in my bag."

They hurried out into the corridor and were just passing the dressing-up cupboard when Mimi came to a halt. Something shiny had caught her eye...

"What's that?" asked Molly, crouching down to pick it up.

"Hey, it's mine," said the cat, swishing her tail angrily.

"Wow!" said Molly with a grin. "It's the key to the dressing-up cupboard! At last I can have a look inside. I'm sure there'll be something special in there I can use to finish off my costume with."

Molly placed the key in the lock and slowly opened the door.

The interior was dark and musty. Molly and Mimi were about to step inside when...

WOOOOAAA

A dark figure with a huge head leaped from the cupboard.

"Rrrreeooooow!"

yowled Mimi and flew off down the corridor.

The figure staggered towards Molly, waving its arms. "I am ICE CREAM JOHNNY THE GHOST-BOY!" it howled.

Molly ran for it.

"Scaredy-cat!" sneered the figure, as Molly disappeared round the corner. "Ha! That showed them. Nobody gets one up on Saffron Von Volavon."

But when she tried to remove her mask it was stuck fast.

"Hang on! Come back," Saffron cried. "Get this thing off me!"

"Mimi, where are you? Miiiimmmiii," called Molly, as she wandered up and down the corridor. She had searched the entire school for Mimi, but with no luck. Where would a terrified cat hide?

In the distance she heard the village clock strike two.

Oh no, the Pet Parade is about to start, thought Molly. *I guess I won't have a pet for it after all.*

She hurried back to the classroom, where the children were putting on their costumes.

"Class, we need to go through to the hall now. The pets are ready and waiting for you backstage," said Mrs Grey.

"Molly, do you want to put on your costume?" asked Jane.

"Mimi's run away," said Molly. "I've looked for her everywhere, but she's totally disappeared. I don't think I'll be able to take part in the Pet Parade."

"But you *have* to," said Jasmine. "Me and Jane finished off your costume for you." She held out a pair of white cat ears and a fluffy white tail.

"You can share Bongo with me," said Jane. "And then we can help you look for Mimi afterwards."

"Thanks," said Molly, putting on the cat ears with a smile.

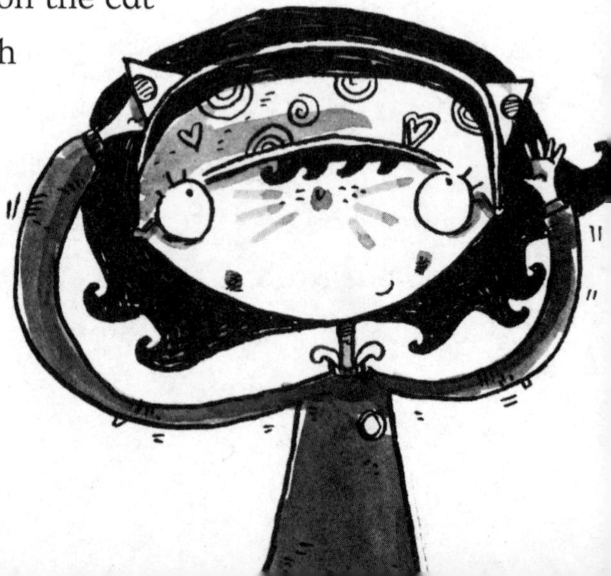

The Show Must Go On

The school hall was bustling with mums and dads, and the pupils and teachers of Fuffleton Primary. The lights dimmed and the hall fell silent.

Mrs Grey stepped on to the stage. "Ladies and gentlemen, boys and girls, may I introduce ... the Fuffleton Primary Pet Parade!"

The music started up. There was a

round of applause and everyone held their cameras at the ready.

A spotlight shone on Misty the rabbit. The rabbit looked rather startled. The spotlight moved from Misty to Jasmine, dressed in bunny ears and a fluffy tail. Jasmine picked up Misty, skipped to the end of the stage and did a neat curtsey. The audience clapped and cheered.

The procession of children and pets began to march out. The mums and dads, pupils and teachers clapped along and cameras flashed.

"This had better be good," hissed Mrs Von Volavon under her breath. "I'm missing my favourite soap!"

"Vivian," snapped Mr Von Volavon. "Will you shut up for once!"

Molly watched from the curtains as her classmates paraded along the stage.

"When's my darling Saffron going to come on?" said Mrs Von Volavon loudly.

"SHHH!" went somebody behind them.

Finally, only Molly and Jane remained behind the curtain. Jane was trying to tempt her sleeping hamster with a peanut.

"And now we have Jane and Bongo ... and Molly and Mimi!" announced Mrs Grey to the sound of applause.

"Yay, Moooollly!" shouted Dad.

Molly was about to follow Jane and Bongo on the stage when she heard a voice behind her.

"What on earth are you wearing?"

"Mimi!" exclaimed Molly. "Where have you been?"

"Never mind that," said Mimi. "There's a Best Pet Prize to win."

Chapter Eleven

Giddy Up, Lady

The crowd went wild as Molly and Mimi took to the stage. Mimi was wearing an enormous puffy ball gown.

Head held high, she padded elegantly across the stage as if it were a catwalk, then did a dramatic spin, revealing the most frilly pair of drawers imaginable.

"Mimi, Mimi, Mimi!" chanted the crowd.

"Thank you, Molly and Mimi," said Mrs Grey, with a beaming smile. "That was ... extraordinary. And now, ladies and gentlemen, boys and girls it's time to award the prize for the Best Pet. So if all our contestants could take to the stage."

The children and pets lined up. "And the winner is..." said Mrs Grey, holding up a gleaming trophy, "Molly and Mimi! For the brilliant idea of having Molly dress as Mimi and Mimi dress as Molly! Well done both of you!"

"WAIT!"

came a voice from the back of the hall. "I haven't had MY turn!"

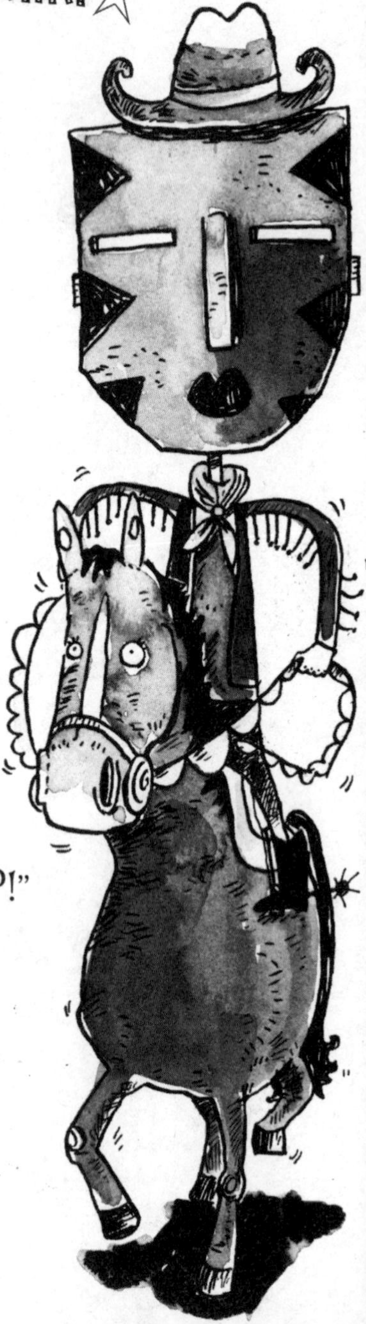

Suddenly a pony trotted through the hall doors. A pony with a very strange-looking rider – a pink cowgirl in a large wooden mask.

Saffron steered Lady between the rows of parents towards the stage.

"Giddy up," said Saffron, but the pony stayed at a walk.

"I said, GIDDY UP!" screamed Saffron at the top of her lungs. "Come ON!"

She gave Lady a sharp kick.

Suddenly, Lady took off at a canter towards the stage. At the last moment, she reared up and did a massive leap.

The children and their pets ran for the curtains.

"Yee-ha!" cried Saffron triumphantly. But as she landed on the stage, her mask slipped down, covering her eyes.

"I CAN'T SEE! Whhooa, Lady!" cried Saffron, attempting to turn the pony round in a circle.

"WHHOOOOA. HEEEELP!"

she screamed, as the pony picked up speed. Suddenly Lady came to an abrupt halt at the edge of the stage, sending Saffron's mask flying through the air, closely followed by Saffron herself.

"Saffron? Where are you?" shrieked Mrs Von Volavon, leaping to her feet.

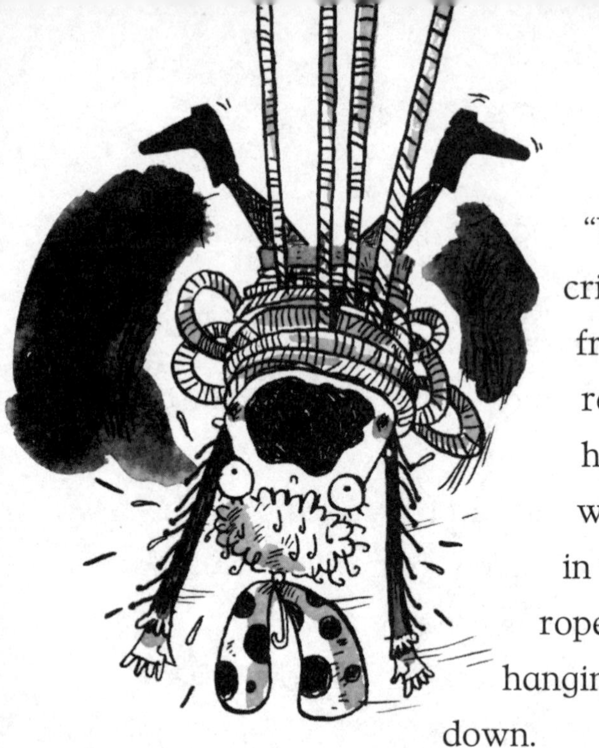

"Up here!" cried Saffron, from the roof of the hall. She was tangled in the gym ropes and hanging upside down.

"MY BABY!" screeched Mrs Von Volavon, as she rushed to stand under her daughter.

"Ahhhhh!" screamed Saffron, as she fell from the ropes. She landed on her mother in a heap.

"Come on, darling! We're going home!" said Mrs Von Volavon, dragging Saffron to her feet. "Clive, go and get that pony!"

Chapter Twelve

Chocolates & Invitations

"Well done, Molly and Mimi!" Mrs Grey handed Molly a gleaming trophy. "Here's the Pet Prize cup, and a box of chocolates! And how can I forget, the prize for your pet," she said, pulling out a bright green rosette. She pinned it to Mimi's collar.

The hall was filled with the sound of claps and cheers.

Molly crouched down to congratulate Mimi. "You look amazing, Mimi," she whispered. "You really deserve the Best Pet Prize."

Mimi shook herself. "Some prize!" she hissed. "Green's SO not my colour."

Molly's parents rushed over. "Molly, I'm so proud of you! When did you have time to make that costume for Mimi?" gushed Mum.

"Well, it just sort of happened," said Molly, not exactly lying.

"Go, Molly!" cried Dad, giving her a big hug.

Brian approached, holding a camera. "Can I take a picture of you and Mimi for the school newspaper?" he asked.

"Of course." Molly grinned and picked up Mimi to pose for the photo. But just then, she caught sight of Saffron hobbling out of the hall.

"I'll be back in a minute..." she said.

"Saffron, wait!" called Molly, catching her up.

"WHAT?" said Saffron. She turned to face Molly with a scowl.

"Would you like a chocolate?" said Molly kindly, holding out the box.

Saffron looked at the chocolates. She picked out a strawberry twirl with a plump pink finger and thumb and popped it in her mouth. A small smile came to her face.

"THH … thhanks…" stammered Saffron, tripping over the unfamiliar word.

"You're welcome," said Molly.

"Well…" whispered Mimi, pawing Molly's arm.

"Saffron," said Molly. "What are you doing tomorrow?"

"Nothing really…" said Saffron in a quiet voice.

Molly smiled. "Would you and Mimi like to come to tea?"

Best
Pet

The FUFFLETON PRIMARY POST

A Purrfect Pair | By Brian Bu

Mimi was the star of the annual Fuffleton Primary Bring Your Pet to School Day on Thursday. The perfect Persian wowed the audience when she took to the stage in a stunning pink ball gown and a very frilly pair of drawers.

“Mimi loves dressing-up – she's a very fashion-conscious kitty,” said her owner, new girl Molly Potsome, modestly.

“Molly's idea of dressing up her cat was a creative triumph,” said teacher Mrs Grey. “Molly has only been at the school for a week, but she is already making her mark at Fuffleton Primary.”

The audience were unaware of the backstage controversy earlier tha

day when

Volavon c

was her

Saffr

perfo

disa

th

I